KB063450

Awakening

Awakening

By Ven. Pomnyun Sunim

Copyright © 2015 By Ven. Pomnyun Sunim
All rights reserved.
Except for brief quotations,
no part of the this book may be reproduced in any form
without a written permission from the publisher.

JUNGTO Publishing
42, Hyoyeong-ro 51-gil, Seocho-gu, Seoul, South Korea / +82-2-587-8991

Website : book.jungto.org

Printed in South Korea
Third Edition : December 2023

Illustration : Boram Lee
Design : Seongsook Yu

ISBN 978-89-85961-98-1 03220

Awakening

By Ven. Pomnyun Sunim

JUNGTO

●

Since I know everything originates from me
And comes back to me
I will practice diligently

We are back on the starting line.

Constrained by all kinds of desires, people rush through their lives in an attempt to satisfy them. The Buddha advised us not to indulge in something today that is likely to give us suffering tomorrow. It's interesting to note how one day, we are so happy with our children, parents, siblings, or friends, but the next day, we are unhappy because of the same people. This is how we live our lives.

We should not live in such a way that we regret and wish to live a different life if we were given a second chance. Furthermore, if the work we are doing now is something that we would stop if we are diagnosed with a terminal illness or face imminent death due to disaster, it means that the work is not meaningfal to us. Even after being told that we have only one month to live, if we want to continue working until we draw our last breath, the work we are doing can be considered truly valuable.

Once time has passed, it never returns. How should we spend these irrevocable moments of our lives? When we reflect on our past, I am sure most of us have many regrettable moments. We blamed our parents for many things and argued with our friends. What do these actions mean in our lives now? Should they really have been the objects of our blame, hate, or argument? Perhaps we wasted valuable time quarreling with and hating the people who didn't deserve such treatment from us?

In retrospect, when was it that you felt content and proud of yourself? Was it when you were looking out for your own interests, or was it when you went out of your way to help your family members or friends? Isn't it true that you remember the time when you were helpful to others as the most proud and rewarding moment? At the end of the day, didn't such a moment actually end up benefiting you the most?

The happy moments in our past often end up making us unhappy, while a difficult time in the past may become a pleasant memory. When we examine our past, we can gain insight into how we should live in the future. We must choose to live a life that is always happy and without regret.

Unwise people with their eyes closed complain that the world is dark. The first thing they should do is to open their eyes. A continuous deep introspection will make it possible. If the world is still dark even after their eyes are open, they should try to light it up. We need to open our eyes first and make the effort to light up the world, which is the meaning of "Attain enlightenment and liberate all unenlightened beings." This is the fundamental teaching that the Buddha imparted to us more than 2,500 years ago.

The past is gone and the future is yet to come. We should be awake each moment and live a cheerful life. Consider your life so far as a practice run for the new life you are about to begin right this moment. Life is precious, but if you idle away your time, it may end up becoming worthless.

In order to live a valuable life, we must first know accurately what a futile life is, so we can discard the worthless pursuits and lead a meaningful life. Then, we can be without regret and be happy every day even if today is the last day of our lives.

Autumn, 2015
Pomnyun

Contents

1

Freedom from Existence

We are no more special

than a clump of grass by the road.

Because we mistakenly believe we are significant,

our lives are filled with suffering,

and ironically, we become insignificant.

Where Are You at This Very Moment?

Don't you think you should know
Where you are going now
And why you are going there?

One afternoon, while napping under a tree, Rabbit was suddenly awakened by a loud thumping sound. Like a bolt of lightning, the thought, "The sky is falling and the ground is caving in," flashed through Rabbit's head, so he began running frantically. Upon seeing this, Deer began to run after Rabbit and asked, "What's the matter? What's going on?"

"The sky is falling and the ground is caving in."

"That can't be true."

"Yes, it's really true."

Considering the possibility that Rabbit could be right, Deer decided to run along with Rabbit. Soon, Fox began running after Deer, Giraffe began running after them, and then Monkey, Elephant, and Raccoon followed suit.

Eventually, all the animals in the forest were running, leaving a big cloud of dust behind them. All the animals ran increasingly faster, thinking that they would have a better chance of survival if they ran ahead of the others. They all strained themselves trying to outrun the others. However, there was a bottomless cliff at the end of the forest. All the animals ran to survive, but in reality, they were running toward their own deaths.

At this sight, Lion, the king of the forest thought, "If they don't stop, they're all going to fall off the cliff and die." So, he jumped in front of the stampede and roared with all his might. Startled by the sound of the loud roar, the animals that had been running in a frenzy came to a sudden halt.

Lion asked, "Where are you all running to?" The animals just stared at one another with no one being able to give an answer.

"What?! You were running as if your lives depended on it, but you don't even know where you were going?" Lion burst out in anger. Then he turned to Raccoon. "Raccoon, why were you running?"

"Elephant was running, so I was just following him."

"What about you, Elephant?"

"Monkey was running…"

Monkey followed Giraffe, Giraffe followed Fox, Fox followed Deer, and Deer followed Rabbit…

At last, Lion asked Rabbit, "Rabbit, why did you run?" Rabbit answered, "I was running away because I thought the sky was falling and the ground was caving in."

"Is it true? The sky is really falling and the ground is caving in? Where did you see that happen?"

"Over where I was taking a nap."

"Really? Well, if that's the case, let's go over there and

take a look."

At Lion's suggestion, all the animals went to the place where Rabbit had been taking a nap. The place, however, looked very peaceful. It did not look like the sky had fallen or the ground had caved in.

"That's strange. I'm certain I heard a loud noise earlier when I was taking a nap…" said Rabbit.

Lion looked around carefully, but all he could see was a tall oak tree and an acorn that had fallen to the ground.

This fable exemplifies the way we live our lives today. We run as if our lives depended on it even though we have no idea where we are headed. Just as Lion stopped the foolish animals from running, the Buddha's teachings give us an opportunity to reflect upon our lives.

Just like the animals running blindly through the forest, we too blindly follow others in our lives. We think that we will lose out on something if we don't run like the others. We strive to stay ahead of the others without realizing that the path we are on leads us to our own demise. Like the animals in a herd, we lead our lives running among a great mass of people, bumping into each other and getting hurt. The injuries from such chaos are the conflicts and unhappiness we experience in our lives now.

Doesn't it make sense to know where we are going and why we're going there? If the path we are on leads to death, we shouldn't follow it even though everyone else does. Even if we have spent a lot of time and energy running along this path, we should just stop and turn around without the slightest hesitation. By doing so, the path to a happy life opens up before us.

Nothing Is Inherently Right or Wrong

If you let go of your stubborn ways,
Your suffering, discriminatory thoughts,
And emotional afflictions will all disappear.
Then, your mind will become clear.

Your present view of life is the product of your environment. Likewise, other people's views are also shaped by their environments. Since everyone has lived in a different environment, each has his or her own unique view of life.

Just as your face looks different from those of others, it is only natural that your opinions will also differ from those of others. Accordingly, if you can accept the fact that everyone is different, the emotional afflictions you experience will significantly decrease. Also, once you realize that nothing is inherently right or wrong and that everyone simply has different opinions, you will no longer insist that only your opinions are correct. If you can put yourself in other people's shoes, you won't have a reason to be in conflict with others.

Your opinions cannot always be right. Similarly, the opinions of others cannot always be wrong. Try to think, "Given his circumstances, it makes sense for him to think that way," or, "I could be wrong." Although you may not perceive the world as it is with enlightened eyes, having this kind of open mind will enable you to feel more lighthearted than before.

One time, a woman came to talk to me about her husband. She wanted to know if I knew of a good way to make her stubborn husband attend a Buddhist temple, so he could listen to the dharma talks and stop being so stubborn. Implicit in her attempt to change her husband was her strong belief that she was right and her husband was wrong.

Therefore, she was determined to do something about her husband's stubbornness.

However, think about how stubborn the wife must be in trying to fix her husband's stubbornness! The wife is actually more stubborn than her husband. When we force our opinion on others, we are the ones who suffer, because no matter how much we assert that they are wrong and that they need to change, they simply will not.

So I suggested to her, "How about if you let go of your belief that your husband is stubborn and instead say to him, 'You are right, honey.'" Often we don't want to give up control or power in a relationship, but in this case, if she lets go of the thought that her husband is wrong, she can be free of her suffering. Since nothing is inherently right or wrong, she can just agree with him by saying, "You are right." Then, her suffering will disappear immediately, and she will feel much better as a result.

If you let go of your stubborn ways of thinking, your suffering will disappear. Therefore, you need to get rid of all your fixed notions. If you don't, attaining enlightenment won't be possible. When you are able to let go, your discriminatory thoughts and emotional afflictions will dissipate, and your mind will become clear.

One Bowl of Rice

False attachment begets grief and fear.
He who is liberated from false attachment feels
Neither grief nor fear.

When a war broke out and people were forced to flee from their homes, a poor farmer set out with a big sack of barley on his back, while a wealthy man got on the road with a bag of gold coins. The wealthy man laughed at the farmer, saying, "Why on earth are you carrying that heavy sack of barley, which is hardly worth anything, when you are fleeing from danger?

On the road, the farmer cooked a small portion of barley to eat for each meal. The wealthy man, however, did not have anything to eat because he carried nothing but gold coins. There weren't any places to buy food either, since everyone was fleeing for their lives.

After starving for a whole day, the wealthy man said to the farmer, "I will give you one gold coin for your sack of barley." One gold coin was worth about five sacks of barley. The wealthy man made the offer as if he were doing the farmer a favor, but the farmer shook his head. The wealthy man burst out angrily, "I know this is wartime, but are you refusing my offer to buy your barley for five times its worth?"

After the second day, the wealthy man became extremely hungry. He proposed to the farmer, "Would you please sell a half sack of barley in exchange for two gold coins?" but the farmer ignored him again.

"It's true this is wartime, but don't you think you are being excessively greedy? How many more gold coins do you want for your barley?"

Another day passed, and the wealthy man was so hungry he couldn't bear it. "I'll give you half of my gold coins for one tenth of your barley."

The farmer still didn't respond, and the wealthy man became furious.

After several days of starvation, the wealthy man became too weak to walk. He felt as if he were about to die of starvation. At that point, his precious gold coins were nothing but a useless, cumbersome burden. Finally, the wealthy man collapsed on the road and implored the farmer. "Please, I am about to die of hunger. Could you hand me a bowl of water so that at least I can have my fill of water before I die?"

Only then did the farmer cook some of his barley and feed the wealthy man.

Freedom from Existence

Existence is neither good nor bad,
Neither pure nor impure.
Thus, there is nothing to attain or discard.

No existence has its own inherently fixed value. We assign values to any existence according to our views and needs at the time. This also applies to what we refer to as "medicine" and "poison." What is the best medicine and what is the most harmful poison for people? Generally, people believe ginseng is medicine and opium is poison. If that is the case, what elements in ginseng and opium make one a medicine and the other a poison?

Our body is made up of diverse elements. Our bodies become ill when it is deficient of a certain element. However, we can become healthy again when that deficiency is supplemented. The substance which supplements the deficient element functions as medicine for the body. On the other hand, when an excessive amount of a particular element has entered the body and has a debilitating effect, the element acts as poison.

Thus, any substance in itself is neither medicine nor poison. It can act as either medicine or poison depending on the situation. Just as a bowl of rice can be helpful like medicine for a hungry person, the same bowl of rice can be harmful like poison for a person who is full.

Accordingly, an object or an incident can be either medicine or poison for you, depending on your current state of mind and situation. By the same token, it may not have any effect on you. Something that everyone in the world considers good could be useless to you. Similarly, something that everyone in the world finds useless and throws away could be just what you need.

You shouldn't take something because you think it's good, and you shouldn't throw something away because you believe it's bad. Likewise, you shouldn't take something because it's clean and throw it away because it's dirty. The existence itself is neither good nor bad and neither pure nor impure. Therefore, there is nothing to attain or discard. This is the key to attaining freedom from existence.

People raise all kinds of thoughts in reaction to their external conditions. Furthermore, they mistakenly believe their thoughts to be objective truths and then attach themselves to the deluded view of reality they have created. Suffering comes from this deluded view of reality. Reality itself is not the source of suffering or fear. It is the delusions about reality that make one suffer and become fearful. Thus, if you are trying to live a happy life, but you are unhappy and life feels hard, this is proof that you have a deluded view of reality.

If you perceive reality as it is, with the eyes of wisdom, you can become free of suffering. In the Heart Sutra (a Buddhist scripture), this concept is expressed as "Cho-Gyeon-Oh-On-Gai-Gong Doh-Il-Che-Go-Aeck," which means that the five fundamentals of human existence – form, sensation, recognition, impulse, and consciousness – in and of themselves are empty by nature. Avalokitesvara Bodhisattva, the bodhisattva of Compassion, was able to free himself of all suffering after seeing clearly that the five fundamentals of human existence are "empty," devoid of inherent qualities.

This means that we can shed all suffering if we can irrevocably realize that all things that exist do not have inherently fixed qualities, so they are neither good nor bad and neither pure nor impure. A person with such a realization is able to do anything in the world.

At This Moment

From moment to moment, we experience life only once,
Whether it is a good day or a bad day.
The sum of all the days makes up our lives.

What do you think freedom is? Generally, people believe freedom is being able to do something when they want to and not do something when they don't want to. Unfortunately, however, the world is not a place where people can do as they please. As a result, people always think their freedom is being restricted.

Is this really true though? The truth is that we are not

restricted by our circumstances. Rather, our tendency to separate "what I like" from "what I don't like" is what restricts our freedom. As long as we are caught up in the notions of "like" or "dislike," we cannot be truly free.

We delude ourselves into thinking that others are restricting us when, in reality, we are restricting ourselves. We have to wake up from this delusion. Just as we can alleviate others from their suffering only when we don't have suffering ourselves, we can help others become free only when we ourselves are free. With the strength we derive from freedom, we can improve ourselves and also make the world a better place.

We have to think it's possible to do anything we want and be anybody we want to be right here and right now. If you think your present situation is unfavorable and spend the day in distress, you have needlessly wasted one valuable day of your life. Every moment of your life is precious and will never come again.

Whether it's a good day or a bad day, each day adds

up to become your entire life. Isn't every day a good day? Unfortunately, people create their own suffering. The source of our unhappiness actually comes from ignoring our reality.

We need to question ourselves, "Are we happy with things as they are?" We should be happy with our lives just the way they are. That way, we won't waste our valuable time and energy making ourselves miserable. Just as the darkness disappears when the lights are turned on, even in the darkest night, we can stop our suffering if we change the way we think about any given situation. Our lives are precious, valuable, and worth living exactly the way they are now.

Even if we are having a hard time now, we should still try to be happy with our lives. We should respect and love ourselves with the proud conviction that we can attain enlightenment and become Buddhas. Taking care of ourselves means neither restricting nor distressing ourselves.

Who can free me and make me happy when I am the one restricting and distressing myself? How can I help others become free and happy when I am in pain myself? First and foremost, I need to become free and happy since everything always starts with me.

Be Happy with Yourself

We create our own happiness.
We create our own unhappiness.
Truly, we create our own happiness and unhappiness.

Although there are countless numbers of bacteria inside our bodies, we still manage to lead relatively healthy lives. Thus, we can safely assume that not all these bacteria cause harm to our bodies. Only when our immune system becomes weak do these bacteria become harmful to our bodies. For example, we don't become infected with the tuberculosis bacteria just because we carry them in our bodies. The tuberculosis bacteria cannot harm healthy bodies.

Then, what about the illness of the mind? When we suffer, we put the blame on someone else, saying things such as, "My child doesn't study. My husband drinks too much. My boss gives me a hard time." We say we are suffering because of somebody or something. We think that in order for us to be free of suffering, the things we disapprove of shouldn't happen. However, if we cultivate our minds well, we won't suffer even if the things we don't like happen to us. This can be compared to having a healthy immune system. When we are healthy, we don't get sick despite the germs inside our bodies.

In order to treat an illness of the mind, we need to know its cause and uproot the source of the problem. The way to eliminate the cause is to realize that the illness did not come from the outside but that we brought it on ourselves. The moment we come to this realization, our illness of the mind can be healed right away and we can be free from suffering.

Therefore, such an illness of the mind is like a dream, frivolous and capricious in nature. Nevertheless, we mistakenly believe that our happiness and unhappiness come from our surroundings, and we relentlessly seek happiness outside of ourselves. Yet, we have no idea how futile such an effort is. Even if we experience happiness from our external conditions, it is not a true or lasting happiness. In fact, it is only a momentary relief from suffering. Soon, the suffering begins anew.

Although suffering has no tangible entity, from moment to moment, we fall into delusion and flounder in the big sea of suffering. There is a simple way to get out of this sea. It is to realize that, inherently, nothing in the world causes suffering.

Repentance

We are no more significant
Than a clump of grass by the road
Because we mistakenly believe we are significant,
Our lives are filled with suffering,
And ironically, we become insignificant.

The most accessible and fundamental treatment for someone with a deep emotional wound is repentance. This is not a process of simply regretting one's wrongdoings but realizing that there is nothing inherently right or wrong in the world. Just as important, repenting makes us realize that we suffer because we perceive and judge things from our subjective views.

Everything originates from us and comes back to us. That is, we are unhappy if we perceive something negatively, while we are happy if we perceive it positively, so ultimately we are the ones who create our own reality. However, we delude ourselves into thinking that others have provided the source of our suffering when it was our own minds that created it. True repentance is clearly understanding and admitting that the suffering originated from our subjective perception.

Self-blame is often confused with repentance. However, the underlying idea of "You were right and I was wrong" is yet another reference to a dichotomic mind that distinguishes between the right and the wrong. In fact, the mind has merely switched the object of blame from others to the self. In the same vein, any grudge you hold against others may not dissipate as long as you firmly believe, "I was right, nevertheless" no matter how many times you prostrate with the aim of repenting. You must realize that nothing is inherently good or bad; they are better or worse only in comparison.

Once we clearly realize that happiness and unhappiness do not depend on outward conditions, nothing in the whole world can have power over us. Since we have control over our own lives, we no longer need to forgive or be forgiven by others. If there is someone we need to forgive, it is because we are still holding onto the thought that we are right. This is an indication that we have a long way to go in our practice and that we are still not awakened from a dream state. We should not hate anyone or believe we need to forgive someone. In truth, there is no one to hate or forgive.

If we feel a sense of injury about something that happens to us, it is because we are not fully aware of the things we have done in our past to bring about such an outcome. Everything originates from us and comes back to us. When we feel a strong sense of injury or resentment arise in our minds, we need to have the wisdom to observe the true cause of these emotions. Therefore, for a practitioner, the time set aside for repentance is crucial. If we repent daily and regularly, the deeply ingrained emotional wounds will begin to heal.

When we despise someone, who is tormented? We are the ones who will end up suffering if we hate someone and get angry. Repentance is a way to cultivate peace of mind and heal ourselves. Repentance is not about discerning who is right and who is wrong; it is realizing that fundamentally there is no right or wrong.

We suffer because we are too attached to the idea "I am right." However, if we realize that there is no intrinsic right or wrong and let go of this idea, our emotional afflictions will disappear immediately. Only then will the path towards peace of mind, happiness, and freedom unfold before us.

Finally, when we practice repentance, the perception that we have been wronged by the world will dissipate. This negative mindset comes from our basic desire to protect ourselves. Ironically, when we regard ourselves as ordinary as a clump of grass by the road, our feelings won't be so easily hurt. However, because we mistakenly believe that we are significant beings, our lives become miserable, and we end up becoming insignificant.

Obstacles That Hinder Practice

Always keep in mind, "I am not anyone special."
The moment you mistakenly believe that you are special,
Life will be miserable.

When asked to sing a song, a person who is not self-conscious will get right up and begin singing any song that comes to his mind, whether it is a children's song or a pop song. However, a self-conscious person will decline, giving an excuse that he cannot sing well. If people keep on insisting that he sing, he will reluctantly do so only after refusing several more times.

Why does he act that way? It's because he is feeling pressured by the thought, "I must perform well." His anxiety, "What if people gossip about my bad singing?" serves as a source for his reluctance. This behavior stems from his self-perception, "I am someone special."

A high social status can actually serve as an obstacle for practice. When the person is repeatedly sought out, respected, and given special treatment by others, he will be deluded into thinking that he is someone very important. Unfortunately, this will only make him even more self-conscious, so he will restrict himself and eventually become unhappy.

Although most of us believe that regarding ourselves as special is crucial to our happiness, if you want to be truly happy, you should always keep in mind, "I am not anyone special." Ironically, you become unhappy the moment you mistakenly believe that you are someone very special just because people seek you out and even idolize you. This is because if you perceive yourself as special, you expect others to treat you as special, and if they don't, you become unhappy. It is better to simply think, "It is their business that they perceive and define me in a certain way," and lead a lighthearted and joyful life.

This can be possible with daily practice. Only by practicing every day can you maintain your mindfulness and promptly let go of any delusions you occasionally fall into. Practice enables you to avoid defining yourself as someone special, thereby allowing you to live a fulfilling life. When you realize that you are not special, no different from a mere wildflower blooming on the roadside, you can be happy regardless of whom you meet, where you go, and what you do in life.

Seeing with an Empty Mind

Just as you simply put down the cup in your hand when it is hot,
When you realize you are in a dream,
You simply need to wake up.

Everything that happens is just an occurrence, so there are no inherently right or wrong values in the phenomena themselves. Something, in itself, does not cause suffering. It is our minds that, upon seeing it, react with emotions such as joy or distress. That is why we should always be mindful.

Then, what should we do when negative emotions, such as anger or sense of injustice, arise? Even when you resolve not to have negative emotions, they will still stir up within you. When you begin to experience feelings of injustice or anger, you need to observe your mind and realize that you are the one who created those emotions. If such emotions have already arisen, simply accept the fact that these emotions have manifested within you.

When you become distressed, it is important to become aware that the emotion is arising within you. However, once you have already become distressed, just accept that you have. Denying that the negative emotion has occurred within you will not take you back to the state before you were distressed. Such an attempt will only lead to additional suffering.

Inherently, nothing is neither good nor bad. Even when you happen to get trapped in your way of thinking and become very angry, you need to first be aware of it and accept your emotion. If you don't fully acknowledge and accept what happens, it becomes harder for you to be aware of the present moment, resulting in further suffering. Always be awake to the present moment.

How can this be achieved? Buddhism emphasizes "just doing something" without a specific condition or purpose. Only when you just do it, when you are awake to the present moment, will the cycle of happiness and suffering be broken. Otherwise, the cycle will continue. How much longer do you want to perpetuate this cycle?

When you realize that the cup you are holding is hot, you simply need to put it down. Similarly, when you realize that you are dreaming, you should simply wake up. No preparation is needed. You just act on it immediately. In short, you need to become aware of the emotions arising within you and let go of them right away.

Whether you do it or not is up to you. It is a matter of choice how you want to live your life. If you like the way you live now, it's perfectly fine to continue to live your life as you have. However, you need to be aware that your present situation is the culmination of the choices you have made thus far. Therefore, you should not complain about your life.

2
Your Life Is Already in Front of You

Becoming the master of your own life begins with the realization,

"I am solely responsible for my life."

If you resolve to take responsibility for your own life,

you already took one step forward on the path to Buddhahood.

Prayer

True prayer is
Letting go of your burning desire.
If you do, you don't need to prostrate
Before a statue of the Buddha until your knees hurt.

What makes us unhappy now? Are we unhappy because of our desire to live in a better house, to have more money, and to attain a higher social status than others, are not being fulfilled? Why do we need so much money and such a big house?

Suffering is caused not only by material things but also by people. You feel unhappy because of your parents, children, friends, lovers, or spouses. When you want to embark on a new venture which your parents do not support, you are in a dilemma because it is very difficult to go against their wishes. Since your parents love you and have given you so much, you feel too indebted to speak your mind. However, the Buddha taught us that in order to break free from the bondage of suffering, we first need to let go of our strong emotional attachments to our spouses, children, and parents.

If someone accidentally grabs a heated iron ball because it looks pretty, he will instantly drop the ball, shouting, "Ouch, it's hot." In this situation, people are torn between wanting to keep the hot iron ball and wishing that the ball weren't hot. Because of their strong desire to keep the iron ball, they will toss the hot ball to the other hand rather than just drop it to the ground. Unfortunately, while one hand may no longer be hot, the other hand will get burned.

Shifting the hot object from one hand to the other does not fundamentally eliminate suffering. The moment we think that we are free of one kind of suffering, we are faced with another. Also, the suffering gradually worsens with time.

People go to Buddhist temples to pray, seeking relief from the suffering caused by problems with their parents, spouses, and children. As such, they are in a state of constant suffering and continue to visit the temple throughout their lives.

However, it is useless to pray if you hope that praying will solve all your problems. True prayer is extinguishing your desires. If you can do that, you will not need to prostrate laboriously before a statue of the Buddha until your knees hurt. Unless you lay down your desires, the suffering will inevitably continue.

Then why do desires arise in us, and why can't we let them go? It is because of the three poisons of the mind – greed, anger, and ignorance. People believe they are happy when good things happen to them and are unhappy when misfortune befalls them. However, everything that happens to them is actually the result of their own actions.

Just as sound is produced when we clap our hands, when our six sense organs – eyes, ears, nose, tongue, body, and mind – interact with external objects, we feel sensation in our bodies, and our minds react accordingly. A sound does not exist on its own. It is generated only when two objects hit against each other.

When the six sense organs in our bodies interact with the external environment, sensations arise in us, which in turn produce the feeling of like or dislike in our minds. Typically, we tend to pull things we like close to us and push things we dislike away from us. These tendencies make up our karma, which in turn creates new desires in us. This cycle is habitually repeated and controls our lives.

Have You Ever Seen a Stone Float on Water?

We are not sent to Heaven or Hell by others.
Neither do we become happy nor unhappy because of others.

A young disciple, Gamini, came to see the Buddha and asked, "Lord Buddha, Brahmans say that when they pray for a person, he will be reborn in a good place after death. They say that even if a person has done bad deeds during his life, he will be forgiven and will be sent to Heaven if a Brahman prays for him with offering to the gods. Is that true?"

"Gamini, did the Brahmans say that? I have something to show you, so follow me."

The Buddha led Gamini to a pond. He picked up a stone and threw it into the pond. "Gamini, what happened to the stone?"

"It sank to the bottom of the pond."

"Let's say Brahmans surrounded this pond and prayed, 'Stone, float to the surface! Please float to the surface!' would it float to the surface?"

"No. It wouldn't."

"Why is that?"

"A stone is heavy, so it naturally sinks to the bottom of the pond."

"That is right. It is natural that a heavy object sinks to the bottom of the pond. Likewise, if a person carelessly takes life, steals the possessions of others, commits sexual misconduct, lies, and has misguided ideas, he will accumulate dark and heavy karma, which, like the stone, will naturally sink to the bottom into Hell. No matter how much Brahmans pray to the gods, it does not help a person go to Heaven."

Then, the Buddha threw a large jar of oil into the pond

and smashed it with a long stick. The oil in the jar spilled out and floated on the surface of the pond.

"Gamini, what is happening?"

"The oil is floating on the surface of the water."

"Let's say Brahmans surrounded the pond and prayed, 'Oil, sink to the bottom of the pond! Please sink to the bottom of the pond!' Will the oil sink?"

"The oil will not sink."

"Why is that?"

"It is the law of nature that light substances float, so the oil won't sink no matter how much one prays."

"That is right. Therefore, if a person is careful not to harm living beings, does not steal from others, does not commit sexual misconduct, does not lie, and does not harbor misguided notions, that is, if a person saves lives in danger, gives to the poor, tries to alleviate the suffering of others, tells the truth, and has wise ideas, his karma will be pure and light. Therefore, like oil, his spirit will naturally rise up and go to Heaven."

The Principle of Cause, Condition, and Effect

You cannot avoid the consequences
Of your accumulated causes and conditions,
Even if you hide at the bottom of the ocean or deep in the mountain.

Your suffering does not occur by itself. It comes from your accumulated causes and conditions, including those you inherited from your parents, those that started when you were inside your mother's womb, those that developed during your early childhood and adolescence, and those that have just been created. The consequence of all of these cumulative causes and conditions are manifested in your present state.

Therefore, even if you are not a Buddhist, if you truly understand that what you are experiencing now is the result of accumulated causes and conditions, there is nothing to fear in this world.

A stone sinks in water, but oil floats on water. According to the law of nature, anything denser than water will sink, but anything less dense will inevitably float. Old sayings such as, "An onion will not produce a rose" and "As a man sows, so he shall reap" express the laws of nature or the principle of cause, condition, and effect.

The principle of cause, condition, and effect is one of the fundamental laws of nature. Whether or not you are aware of it, acknowledge it, or believe it, this principle exists and applies to all of us. Expecting a good outcome after doing bad deeds goes against this law. It is also as foolish to expect a rose to bud after planting an onion as is to wait for a stone to float on water or for oil to sink under water.

In the principle of cause, condition, and effect, the cause refers to the direct cause of the effect, whereas the condition refers to the indirect cause. For example, a seed is considered a direct cause while soil, fertilizer, sunlight, and air are considered indirect causes. As the seed can germinate only after being exposed to soil, water, and air, the direct and indirect causes must come together to create an effect.

Even on the most fertile soil, nothing can sprout without a seed. On the other hand, even the healthiest seed cannot germinate without soil. Only when direct and indirect causes are combined, can the effect be created. Sometimes, the direct cause may have more influence on the effect than the indirect cause, or vice versa. But without either one of them, there will be no effect.

Interconnectedness of Every Existence in the World

You and I, we are interconnected with each other at all times.
You cease to be when I cease to be
I cease to be when you cease to be.

The validity of the principle of cause, condition and effect comes from the very fact that this world is based on the Law of Dependent Origination. This law can be explained as the following: "This exists because that exists, and that exists because this exists," "This is created because that is created," or "This ceases to exist because that ceases to exist." The Law of Dependent Origination provides the basic tenets of the principle of cause, condition, and effect.

To lead a happy life, we need to accurately understand the Law of Dependent Origination. For instance, it is only natural that good deeds entail good consequences and that bad deeds bring harsh retributions. Therefore, we need to fully comprehend how the law functions.

A child is interconnected with his or her parents, a husband with his wife, and a teacher with his or her students. We are always interconnected with others. That is, you cannot exist by yourself, and I cannot exist by myself either.

When the causes and conditions of a man and a woman are combined, he becomes a husband and she becomes a wife. By the same token, when the man and the woman part from each other due to divorce or death, he is no longer a husband and she is no longer a wife. A man's body by itself is not a husband. Only in association with his wife can he be a husband, and only when he has a child, can he become a father.

The physical body itself has no inherent nature that is

permanently independent and immutable. Self-nature is manifested in relation to others but disappears when that relation ceases. This is the essence of the Law of Dependent Origination.

The sprouting of a seed or the birth of a baby are just the results of causes and conditions. The combination of causes and conditions creates a new form, but when the combination dissolves, the form disappears and returns to "emptiness."

A man and a woman become husband and wife based on certain causes and conditions, and they maintain their interconnectedness for a period of time. However, just like water, which is created from the chemical reaction of hydrogen and oxygen and maintains its form only for a fixed period of time, the relationship of a husband and a wife does not last forever. Throughout our lives, we live according to the causes and conditions we have created. Every existence in the world, including our bodies and thoughts, appear and disappear according to this principle.

Good Causes and Conditions, Bad Causes and Conditions

It may seem that
There are good causes and conditions
And bad causes and conditions in life.
However, there are no such distinctions on the path to enlightenment.

Let's say there is a bean. While this bean is not likely to germinate if it drops on a desk or in sand, it will germinate well when it lands on fertile soil. Thus, it is important to have good causes and conditions to obtain desirable results, so we should try our best to attract them.

However, it's not so easy to encounter good causes

and conditions from the beginning. In the eyes of unenlightened beings whose judgment is clouded by greed, fertile land looks like a waste land, and a neatly grooved sandy field devoid of compost looks clean and attractive. As a result, people often plant the seed in the wrong place. Their lives resemble those of mice going after poison-laden food that looks and smells delicious. In short, people's lives are driven by their greed to attain good looks, fortune, power, and honor. Thus, greed is what prevents us from forming good causes and conditions.

Among all the relationships people form, a marital one is the most selfish. People value loyalty when befriending someone and evaluate the level of trust when choosing a business partner. However, when entering into a marriage, they have a countless number of expectations for their prospective spouses.

Because people get married with such greedy and selfish motives, it's hard for them to meet good spouses. Also, because people choose their spouses based on high expectations, they are likely to be disappointed and end up hating each other even over small disagreements. People get married in order to be happy, but in reality, the marriage becomes a source of suffering and unhappiness.

Therefore, before you get married, it is advisable to practice in order to gain deep insight into your mind. Then, it will become easier to cultivate your mind so that you are able to let go of your greed and become more compassionate and understanding.

However, what do we do about the causes and conditions that have already been created? For example, if a bean happened to land on gravel, should we just lament over why it landed there of all places? Of course not. Regardless of the type of soil the bean has landed on, we need to think about how to help it sprout. In other words, we need to work with the given causes and conditions and try to improve the situation as best we can. If the causes and conditions were bad, we should turn them into good ones, and if they were good to begin with, we should make them even better.

When you face bad causes and conditions, you shouldn't say, "There is nothing I can do. I am going to give up." These causes and conditions are obstacles that you need to surmount sooner or later. If you want to attain happiness and freedom, embrace both the good and bad causes and conditions that come your way. The sooner you overcome the unfavorable causes and conditions in your life, the closer you will be to the path to enlightenment.

It may seem that there are good and bad causes and conditions in life, but there are no such distinctions on the path leading to enlightenment. Whether your present causes and conditions are good or bad, you simply need to accept them and improve them. Ultimately, you should strive at all times to create favorable causes and conditions in your life.

Your Life Is Already in Front of You

If you resolve to take responsibility for your life,
You are already one step closer to the path toward Buddhahood.

Before the advancement of science, it was quite common for fishermen to lose their lives in the stormy sea. These days, however, because fishing ships do not set sail until after checking the weather forecast, the incidence of such accidents has decreased significantly. Even though we may not be able to stop the tidal waves or severe storms, we can now predict them and take the necessary precautionary measures. Thus, our fear of natural disasters has been greatly reduced.

Likewise, once you understand the law of cause, condition, and effect, you can predict the consequences of having a certain mindset or attitude. This will enable you to avoid creating the causes or conditions that will bring you suffering. Also, when you have already formed certain causes and conditions, you can face the consequences resolutely, since you understand you will have to face them sooner or later.

Your life is already in front of you. Therefore, you should be ready to accept and embrace all your problems and agonies. Even a difficult relationship with someone due to negative causes and conditions can be improved if you regard that person with a bodhisattva's compassion. You can change the causes and conditions since nothing in the world is predetermined and permanent.

When people are unhappy with their lives, they tend to blame the people around them such as their parents, spouses, or children. They believe their own happiness or unhappiness is dependent on the actions of these people. However, becoming the master of your own life begins with the realization, "I am solely responsible for everything. All the things that happen in my life are the consequences of the causes and conditions I have created." If you resolve to take responsibility for your own life, it means you have already taken one step forward on the path to Buddhahood. No matter what hardships you may face, you must realize, "I am solely responsible for this since it is the result of the causes and conditions I have created." This is the mindset of a bodhisattva.

When praying, your intention should not be to gain something, but rather to reflect on yourself. Only then will the obstacle in front of you disappear. Once the obstacle is removed, you can clearly see your true nature and will be able to solve any problems you face.

Being able to see your true nature or your karma is as good as finding the solution to your suffering. Now, it's up to you whether or not you decide to improve your karma and take actions to free yourself from suffering.

For example, people who are not aware that they are living in a low-lying terrain cannot protect themselves from water damage when there is a flood. Likewise, the people who know they are living in a low-lying area but neglect to prepare for possible flooding also suffer water damage when there is a flood. However, those who live in the same area but take the time to build levees, raise the ground level of their houses, or relocate, are able to avoid flood damage.

Therefore, it's not important whether you live on high ground or low ground. If your house is on low ground, you can prepare in advance for possible flooding in the future. Even if it begins to rain before all the preparation is done, you can still cope with the situation more easily and safely because you were already aware there would be a flood. In a similar manner, practice can help us become prepared for various unexpected situations in our lives.

Only Wash Hands When You Wash Hands
Only Eat When You Eat

You are no longer an unenlightened being.
You are someone who is going to be a Buddha.
A Buddha shouldn't be living a life filled with worries and trivial conflicts.

If you want to live a full and exciting life, you need to have an open mind. How joyful it is to live in this world! You may live your life as if you were hiking up a mountain. You can freely explore different valleys while hiking through the mountain of your life. Instead, you enclose yourself in your own limited perspective of the world, which makes you miserable.

You should not waste time contemplating where you should go or what you should do. Life should be so much fun that you don't want to miss a beat, even when it throws you a curveball. Only then can you enjoy life to its fullest. Then, when life ends, you will be able to depart this world without any regrets. However, people complain and whine about their miserable lives every day. Yet, ironically, when they approach the end of their lives, they despair because they don't want to die.

We should only wash hands when we wash hands and only eat when we eat. But we often do things the other way around by thinking of food when we wash hands or thinking about washing hands when we eat. Because living in this inverted way brings suffering, we plead to others to help us out of our misery.

We need to make an earnest wish to become a Buddha. We should be mindful of the fact that we are no longer unenlightened beings because we are destined to be Buddhas someday. Should a Buddha be constantly worrying and getting into conflicts with others day after day? We should live a life full of energy with the high aspiration, "I am going to be a Buddha. I will not live a petty and miserable life."

3

The Path to Enlightenment

Reflecting on yourself
is true meditation and true chanting.
Such self-reflection opens up
the path to enlightenment and Buddhahood.

The Path to Enlightenment

Reflecting on yourself
Is true meditation and true chanting.
Such self-reflection opens up the path to enlightenment and Buddhahood.

One day, Mazu Daoyi was meditating. His teacher, Nanyue Huairang, who had been walking by, stopped to ask him a question. "What are you doing?"

"I am meditating"

"Why are you meditating?"

"I want to become a Buddha."

Upon hearing the answer, the teacher brought over a

brick. He sat next to his disciple and began polishing it.

Curious, Mazu Daoyi asked, "Teacher, what are you doing?"

"I am trying to make a mirror."

"How can you make a mirror by polishing a brick?"

"How can you attain enlightenment by meditating?"

"Then, what do I need to do?"

"If an oxcart stops moving, should you whip the cart or the ox?"

At that very instant, Mazu Daoyi attained enlightenment.

The disciple, believing that meditation was the best method for achieving enlightenment, was imitating the act of meditating. However, the teacher made him realize that the actions of "meditation" or "chanting," in and of themselves will not lead to true Buddhahood.

Enlightenment doesn't come from meditation itself. Sincere self-reflection is true meditation and true chanting. Only such deep self-reflection will open up the path to enlightenment and Buddhahood.

Practice in Name Only

What is it to live like this?
And what is it not to live like this?

Most of the time, people are not aware that they are filled with self-contradictions. In fact, they are blinded by delusions so often that they don't realize their own ignorance.

Once, someone came to talk to me about his unhappy life.

"Sunim, I can no longer live my life like this because it's too painful. I'm almost fifty years old. I know I should practice diligently before I get older, but I'm wasting each and every day without doing practice, which is making me really miserable."

So I asked him. "What is it 'to live like this' and what is it 'not to live like this?'"

"'To live like this' is to make money and live an ordinary life, and 'not to live like this' is to focus on practice instead. The fact that I don't practice is making me very unhappy."

I asked, "By the way, why do you want to practice so much?"

"To attain liberation."

"What is liberation?"

"To be free from suffering."

Can you see the contradiction in this dialogue? What is the use of "practice" when people say they feel miserable because they cannot practice or because their practice is not going well? People practice because they want to be free from suffering. However, if they are unhappy because they are unable to practice, how can practice help them become free from suffering? They make practice itself into another source of suffering for themselves.

In this man's case, he had created another source of major suffering for himself while trying to free himself from his original suffering. Unfortunately, he was completely clueless about this self-contradiction. Such practice is practice in name only. Likewise, such liberation is liberation in name only. It has nothing to do with true practice and true liberation.

It Is You Who Makes Someone into a Teacher

Only when you have faith, will you have a teacher.
If you have faith in him,
He immediately becomes your teacher.

A teacher offers many teachings to help students overcome their ignorance. However, a student without faith in his teacher, even after one or two years, is likely to think, "I haven't learned anything yet." Only when you have faith, will you have a teacher.

It is not necessary for someone to have great capabilities in order to become a teacher. If you have faith in him, he becomes your teacher. Even a piece of wood can be a Buddha to you if you regard it as such with unshakable faith. However, without such faith, no matter how great the teacher might be, he is just a powerless, ordinary person to you.

It is possible to experience a miracle even when we regard a wooden Buddha with as much sincerity as we would the Shakamuni Buddha. Imagine what kind of miracle we may witness when we can reflect on ourselves humbly in front of a real living human being as if he were the Buddha. We would be rewarded with abundant blessings. Yet, people are reluctant to take the actions that will bring miracles and blessings.

How is it that you can bow down to a stone Buddha statue but not to your parents, husbands, wives, or children? If you are able to regard a piece of carved stone as the Buddha, what prevents you from doing the same toward the people in your life?

Even bowing down humbly before a stone Buddha statue with sincere faith can help you change your thoughts and actions, thereby bringing you great blessings. Just imagine how many more blessings you will receive when you practice by reflecting on yourself and on being humble toward your parents, spouses, and children.

When the teacher says, "If you dig here, you will get water," the student should grab a shovel and begin digging without any hesitation. However, a student who has little faith in his teacher will be asking, "Will I really get water if I dig here?" Or, "Are you sure about that?" instead of digging right away. Such weak faith might not bring you any blessings.

You should be able to see the contradiction in asking the teacher for instructions but not following them because you don't trust him. Since you don't have faith in your teacher, you repeatedly ask for reassurance. Even when you follow his instructions and put them into action, you begin to doubt and become skeptical, and eventually give up. As a result, you end up needlessly wasting your time and efforts in digging holes here and there without ever finding water.

Things as They Are

Why should we sacrifice the only life we have?
In order to live with no regrets,
We have to see things just as they are.

One day, I asked a visitor who was about to get married, "Why do you want to marry her?" After he gave me several reasons, I told him that he would be better off remaining single.

He retorted jokingly, "Sunim, it's all right that you're not married, but do you have to discourage everyone else from getting married?"

Actually, the reason I told him that he shouldn't get married was because it seemed unlikely that his prospective spouse would be able to provide all the things he wanted in a marriage. So, if he was serious about making his ideal marriage a reality he'd have to marry another woman. If he had his heart set on marrying his fiancée, however, he would need to change his notion of what an ideal marriage is. Since his objective and choice of spouse did not match, I told him not to go through with it.

Should he, then, not even consider such a marriage? No, he shouldn't. Unless he changes his current views, he would be better off living alone. If he were still determined to marry this woman, he'd need to alter his views on marriage. In other words, he needed to be more flexible. He should approach married life with the attitude, "I can't even control my own life. I shouldn't meddle in the life of my future wife and try to control her."

When couples with serious marital problems come to me for counseling, they generally believe they know exactly what I will say. They assume that a Buddhist monk would never advise them to divorce but instead will say, "Look, you have to save the marriage at all costs," or, "You need to put up with each other."

On the contrary, I would never say such a thing. I've chosen the single life for myself. Why on earth would I pressure anyone else to stay married? Believing that everyone else should either get married or stay single is a biased view.

In general, most people who are considering divorce are worried about their children and harbor a deep-seated resentment toward their spouses. Also, it is rare that one party is solely responsible for the conflicts that lead to divorce.

When people get divorced while worrying about their children, feeling resentment toward their spouse, or are immersed in self-contradictory thoughts, they will regret their decision. They must face the inevitable difficulties that accompany divorce. Life unavoidably becomes more miserable as these regrets deepen.

Before getting divorced, you should look deep into your heart. After you have taken everything into consideration and have reached the conclusion that you can no longer sustain your marriage, only then is it alright to get a divorce. That's because everyone gets married with the intention of becoming happy, not the opposite. However, before making a final decision, you must be able to view your own marriage as objectively as possible, as if you were looking at someone else's marriage. You shouldn't make assumptions and judge your spouse according to your value system. Furthermore, you shouldn't make yourself miserable by drawing negative conclusions about your spouse based on your own suppositions.

In order to view your spouse objectively, you have to put yourself in his or her shoes. The husband should try to consider things from his wife's point of view, and vice versa. Now, I'm not saying you should unconditionally support your spouse's position and endure everything. Why should you sacrifice the only life you have? You need to perceive things objectively, just as they are. This will enable you to make wise decisions and live your life without regrets.

This principle applies to more than just marital relationships. When you have conflicts with your parents, friends, or coworkers, try to see things from their perspective. You can never be objective unless you put yourself in the other person's shoes. Being objective means letting go of your own views. You should make a judgment only after seeing things in a completely objective way. After this process, if you are able to come to terms and understand your spouse, you can stay in the marriage. However, if you find that you just absolutely cannot compromise on something, then you have to do what it takes to resolve that issue.

Reflect on the Past and Look at the Present from the Perspective of the Future

Seeing with an expansive and long-term outlook
Allows us to gain deep insight into the true nature of reality.

People always look at others from their own point of view and observe things in relation to their own interests. With such a biased perspective, they have difficulty evaluating facts objectively. Before deciding on what action to take, you should try to see things as they are. This is the "Right View," the first factor of the Noble Eightfold Path, which leads to liberation and nirvana.

Imagine it's pouring rain near the top of the river and water is rushing down toward the river's mouth. If the people living around the lower regions believe they will be alright since it's not raining where they are and fail to take any preventive measures, they are bound to be flooded. What is the reality of this situation? Being able to see the state of things as they are means knowing that the rainfall in the upper reaches will soon make the levees downstream overflow.

What should people do after clearly seeing things as they are? In other words, what decisions should they make? Even if there is flooding upstream, those living in the lower regions can evaluate their situation for themselves. If the people of the lower regions know that the levees downstream won't overflow because they have considered all the factors, such as the amount of precipitation, the width and depth of the river, and current water levels in the reservoir, they can remain calm no matter how much fuss everyone else makes.

On the other hand, if they determine that the levees may

overflow, they should raise them, even though everyone else deems it unnecessary. If they decide that the rainfall is too heavy for the levees to hold up, they need to evacuate to higher ground immediately.

We need to have a Right View to live our lives wisely, but that's not enough. In addition to seeing things as they are, we also need to have the right perceptions. This is called "Right Thought." Right View and Right Thought together are known as wisdom.

What is practice? It's a way to live wisely. People become fixated on thoughts such as, "I'm better than others," or "I am right," which prevents them from seeing things as they are. Blinded by their self-centeredness, they make erroneous judgments and act foolishly. Practicing repentance by prostrating with a humble mind and repeating to oneself, "I am sorry I believed I was right," lessens the sense of self-importance that makes them assert, "I am right."

Practice is placing ourselves in the shoes of people we cannot possibly understand and calmly pondering why they cannot help behaving in a certain way, considering what it must have been like for them growing up, and observing their present state of mind.

When we understand others through this process, we feel less frustrated. Furthermore, when we fully understand them and have compassion for them, we may even be able to help them solve their problems.

If, on the other hand, we can't understand others because we are too preoccupied with our own thoughts, continue to assert our own opinions, and try to change others, everyone involved will end up frustrated, and nothing will get resolved. Unfortunately, in our lives, we often behave in such foolish ways.

Being awake to the present moment at all times is very difficult. When something happens, we are unconsciously dragged into the situation, realizing and regretting our behavior only in hindsight. There are many incidents that seemed like a big deal at the time but feel very trivial later. We can, therefore, assume that whatever enormous adversity we now face may turn out to be insignificant at some point in the future. In other words, by looking back on our past, we can correctly assess the present situation from the perspective of the future.

Additionally, incidents that we feel are a big deal may appear inconsequential from a third person's point of view. Therefore, we should view things that happen to us as if they were happening to someone else. Simply put, we need to look at things both from a broad and long-term perspective. When we become preoccupied by our own thoughts or gripped by the situation at hand, we become shortsighted. Also, when we make decisions based on only one aspect of things, chances are that we will end up seriously regretting them.

In all circumstances, we need to have a broad as well as a long-term perspective that includes insight into other people's situations. That is, we should not look at things solely based on our own subjective interests. Only when we view things correctly, can we have the right perception. For example, when we are buttoning up our shirts, if we start off with a button in the wrong hole, the rest of the buttons will certainly end up in the wrong holes. In sum, the most important purpose of studying the Buddha's teachings lies in having the right perception. This is the fundamental basis for living right.

Why Love Turns into Hatred or Sorrow

Do I truly understand those around me?
Am I forcing them to follow my ways?

A child caught a crab in a brook and pulled one of its legs off. The other children who were playing with him happily cheered him on. Encouraged by his friends' excitement, the child pulled the rest of the legs off, threw the legless crab back into the brook, and was about to do the same to another crab.

At this sight, the Buddha asked the children, "How would you feel if someone pulled your arms or legs off?"

"Well, it would hurt a lot."

"And how would your mom, dad, brothers, and sisters feel if they saw someone pulling your arms or legs off?"

"They would be very sad."

"That's right. Crabs have moms, dads, brothers, and sisters, too. Imagine how sad the other crabs would feel if they saw a fellow crab with all of its legs missing?"

The children finally realized just how horrible their behavior had been.

"We are very sorry. We did it out of ignorance. Buddha, we promise we won't ever do it again."

The Buddha responded, "It is all right if you realize that what you did was wrong. Now that you know, it's important that you never do it again."

In this story, the Buddha imparted the teaching that people inflict pain not only on themselves but also on others out of ignorance. Though the creature may be a mere crab, understanding its suffering is important. Love should always accompany understanding.

What can we say about love nowadays? We mostly see love that is based on possessiveness, greed, and self-centeredness rather than one that is based on understanding. This kind of love can easily turn into hatred or sadness at any moment. When the people we love don't fulfill our expectations, or when we can't have our way with them, love can instantly turn into hatred.

So why does love turn into hatred or sadness? It is because such love is rooted in our desire to possess the other person the way we want instead of trying to understand the other person. Again, this kind of love can easily turn into suffering.

We should ask ourselves, do we truly understand those around us? Could we be imposing our own ways on them without realizing it?

4

Those Who Influence Others

A wet rag cleans the floor by soaking up all the dirt.
Likewise, those who influence their surroundings
absorb and cleanse the bad habits and negative behaviors
of other people and change them for the better.

Those Who Are Easily Influenced by Negative Conditions

People feel they need to go to college because others go to college
And that they need to buy cars just because others buy cars.
We think we're leading independent lives,
But we are actually copying what others are doing without even realizing it.

People can be divided into four different categories depending on the way they respond to negative external conditions. The first category is made up of those easily influenced by negative conditions. The second category is made up of people who deliberately distance themselves from negative conditions so that they can remain unaffected.

In the third category are those who manage to remain unaffected even when surrounded by negative conditions. Finally, the last category consists of those who are not only unaffected by the negative conditions but also influential in transforming the unfavorable environment into a favorable one.

What kind of people are those who are influenced by external conditions? They are those who, when living with a friend who drinks, unconsciously begin to drink themselves. If they live with a person who gets angry easily and uses foul language, they become short-tempered and also begin swearing. Additionally, living with lazy and greedy people, they too become lazy and greedy. They unconsciously imitate the bad habits of others around them just like the way their clothes get damp in the fog before they are aware of it.

Ordinary people are easily affected by negative conditions. When they are asked why they acquired the bad habits, they respond, "Do you think I wanted to? I got these bad habits just by living with them." We end up doing what others around us do. We go to school because others do. Then, we get a job and get married simply because others do so.

Young adults who did not drink in high school begin drinking and smoking cigarettes when they go to college because they see their friends doing these things. They emulate these behaviors simply because they feel the pressure to conform. Also, if our co-worker buys a house or a new car, we feel pressured to do the same. People seem to lead independent lives, but actually they tend to follow the actions of others quite unconsciously. Those who blindly follow the actions of others are called "unenlightened beings," or ordinary people.

Individuals reported in the media for corruption often defend themselves vehemently. They argue that since their predecessors did the same, they thought their actions were acceptable. They are not particularly bad people. They simply followed the examples of their predecessors. That's why these people hardly feel any guilt. When they are being investigated, they feel they are unjustly accused and complain, "Everybody does it but gets away with it. Why am I so unlucky?"

In general, ordinary people are easily influenced by external conditions. There is an anecdote about a famous Chinese Confucius philosopher, Mencius, which illustrates this point. Mencius's mother moved three times in search of an ideal environment for her son's education. Given both good and bad influences, people are more susceptible to the latter. People have a tendency to learn bad habits more quickly. However, this doesn't mean that learning positive behavior is particularly difficult. When everyone around us behaves in a positive way, we can learn positive behaviors just as easily.

Those Who Are Not Influenced Because They Distance Themselves from External Conditions

We like one person for certain reasons
And dislike another for certain reasons.
These opposite emotions are fundamentally the same,
Since both feelings are rooted in our desires.

In the second category are the people who are not influenced by negative external conditions because they distance themselves from them. They don't associate with friends who drink or smoke. They don't live with people who use foul language. All in all, they sever ties with people with bad habits and avoid associating with them. They behave like the saying, "He that touches pitch shall be defiled." People in this category avoid anything or anyone that can influence them negatively. Because these people don't demonstrate any bad habits or negative behaviors, they are described as "pure, and noble." Buddhist monks generally fall into this category.

The people in the first category highly respect those in the second category, to the point that the former group deifies and idolizes the latter. However, despite their respect and admiration, the people in the first category do not follow the example of those in the second. When asked why they don't, they answer, shaking their heads, "How can people live like that?" Still, they greatly admire those in the second category. Although the people in the first category do not want to live like those in the second category, they expect others to do so. They explain the reasons they don't do it themselves by saying, "If everyone lived like that, the world would not go around." It's as if they continue their bad habits and negative behaviors out of concern for the world.

Fundamentally, however, the people in the first two

categories can be considered to be the same in the sense that they are in danger of being influenced by external conditions. Whether they accept or reject the external circumstances, both groups are dependent on them. While the people in the first category are bound by the belief, "I have to live like others," those in the second category are equally bound by the idea, "I must not live like others." In other words, those in the first group are trapped by their desire, and those in the second group are trapped by their determination to shield themselves from external conditions. The people in the first category are fenced in by the thought, "What's the fun of living if people don't eat meat and drink alcohol?" while those in the second category are restricted by the notion, "I must not eat meat or drink alcohol."

Generally, we say, "I love this person because of this and that reason, but I hate that person for such and such reasons." Although these are opposite feelings, they are fundamentally the same in the sense that they are both based on desire. People are happy when their desires are satisfied and unhappy when they are not. Love and hate spring from the same root and are like two sides of the same coin.

Those Who Are Not Influenced by External Conditions

Those who are free because they are no longer attached to their desires,
Those who are not influenced by circumstances,
They are Mahayana bodhisattvas.

Those who do not try to avoid but remain unaffected by their surrounding conditions are the people who are not influenced by external conditions. They don't drink or smoke, even when they are with their friends who do. Also, they don't become greedy despite living among such people.

Only when people reach this stage can they talk about

being "free." Because people in the third category are unaffected by desires, they are free from external conditions. Since they are unmoved by any external condition, they are not influenced by any situation they find themselves in. They are called Mahayana bodhisattvas

Figuratively speaking, the people in the first category are those who go out to sea on a boat, are washed overboard by big waves, and frantically call for help while struggling to stay alive. They are the people who have conflicts with their parents who have raised them. They are the ones who married someone they loved but soon become unhappy in their marriages, who get angry at their children because they fall short of their expectations, and who clash with their co-workers at work. The way people become angry, irritated, resentful, distressed, and lonely in their relationships with others is no different from the way people cry out for help while trying to stay afloat after falling overboard into the sea.

The people in the second category can be compared to those who have built a levee to keep out the waves and enjoy riding the boat safely on calm waters. They are those who suffered deeply in their lives and one day realized the futility of leading such an unhappy life. Consequently, they sever all family and social ties and live in the mountains or deep in the woods. Since they cut off all ties, they no longer suffer because of work or people. They say, "Now, no one can bother me. My mind is at peace." However, their lives can be compared to rowing a boat on a tranquil lake, trapped inside a levee. They are not really free.

The people in the first category experience a momentary happiness between waves. When a wave hits, they are immersed in the sea. Then, when the wave passes, they can raise their heads to the surface and breathe. They feel happy for an instant before another wave hits them. Similarly, in life, people alternately experience suffering and happiness from moment to moment.

The people in the second category also alternate between suffering and happiness. However strong the levee may be, it will eventually break if big waves continuously crash into it. Even if the levee does not break, the reality is that they are trapped inside and cannot get out. They enjoy limited freedom inside the levee, but that is not true freedom.

The people in the third category build a big boat and learn to skillfully navigate the sea by making full use of the given conditions of the wind and the waves. Unhindered by the capricious weather, they sail the seas to their hearts' content. If it's windy, they sail the boat using the force of the wind. Similarly, if the waves are big, they use the power of the waves to sail the boat. They are unaffected by any external conditions. Some people may believe that these people have attained complete freedom or nirvana. However, they have yet to attain absolute happiness or freedom.

Those Who Influence Their Surroundings

It is good when they fall into the sea
And it is also good when they don't.
They are happy whether or not they fall into the sea.

The people in the first, second, and third categories have one thing in common. Those in the first are suffering because they have fallen into the sea against their will. Those in the second have built a levee so that they won't fall into the sea. Finally, those in the third are on a big boat, freely sailing the seas despite strong winds and high waves. What all three categories share is that they believe they must avoid being thrown into the sea in order to be happy.

There is a fourth and last category of people who are quite different from those in the first three categories. What kind of people are those in the fourth category? These are the people who do not give much thought to "not falling into the sea." Also, they don't mind even if they do fall into the sea. The people in the first three categories believe that they can never be happy if they fall into the sea. However, those in the fourth category are happy whether or not they do. What do these people do when they happen to fall into the sea? They collect pearl oysters since they are already there. Shellfish divers dive into the sea to collect clams or sea cucumbers, while adventurers do it to look for treasure from sunken ships. When they dive for sea cucumbers and pearl oysters, divers have not unintentionally tumbled into the sea but have gone below water to do their jobs.

If by chance the people in the fourth category are thrown overboard while sailing, they will gather some clams while they are under the sea. Falling into the sea is not a stressful and unpleasant experience for them. Just as those who deliberately dive into the sea for a purpose, they feel they might as well take advantage of their situation by picking up some clams while there. They are truly free because they are happy whether or not they fall into the sea.

To reiterate, the people in the first category are those who repeatedly make mistakes even though they try not to. Those in the second, to ensure that they do not fail, choose not to do anything. Those in the third don't make any mistakes no matter what they do.

Finally, those in the fourth don't mind whether or not they make a mistake because they learn even more when they make a mistake than they would when they don't mess up. They recognize that something that is thought to be an adversity usually turns out to be a blessing in disguise. You need to understand this fourth category to be able to comprehend the meaning of enlightenment or nirvana achieved by the Buddha.

To a casual observer, it is virtually impossible to

distinguish between the people in the first category and those in the fourth. The people in the second category are completely different from those in the first, so it is easy to tell them apart. Those in the third category might be a little hard to distinguish from those in the first because they live in the same environment. However, upon closer observation, it is easy to separate them because those in the third category are special. They don't get angry when someone swears at them, and they do not drink even when they hang out with people who do. They mix and mingle with others like friends but something about them makes them stand out as special and extraordinary. However, the people in the fourth category behave virtually in the same way as those in the first, making them almost impossible to tell apart.

The people in the fourth category are not afraid of being influenced by the negative conditions surrounding them. Moreover, they don't consider being uninfluenced as their ultimate goal either. They live among "unenlightened beings," and make a positive impact on everything they touch, making the world a more beautiful place to live in.

Using another analogy to elaborate on the differences, the people in the second category don't befriend anyone who drinks while those in the third category don't mind friends who drink, but they themselves don't drink. What about those in the fourth category? They hang out with friends who do and drink along with them, so it's quite impossible to distinguish them from the rest.

But, after a while, surprisingly, their drinking buddies stop drinking. In a similar vein, when a woman in this category lives with a husband who uses foul language, she also uses foul language toward him, but after some time has passed, the husband unconsciously stops swearing. When people in the fourth category live with greedy people, the latter group becomes less greedy. Also, when they befriend delinquents, they misbehave along with them, but after a while, the latter group of people somehow becomes reformed.

A wet rag cleans the floor by soaking up all the dirt.

Likewise, the people in the fourth category absorb and cleanse the bad habits and negative behaviors of other people and change them for the better.

True Freedom

True freedom is possible
Only when you have attained enlightenment.

The only way you can have true freedom is by attaining enlightenment. Consequently, cultivating mindfulness cannot be taught by the traditional learning method of modeling. You have to come to the realization on your own.

Attaining enlightenment is not an adaptation to the environment; it is actually similar to mutation. When people change by adapting to the environment, they are likely to change again when there is a change in the environment. Such changes are not passed down to their descendants. However, mutations are permanent trait changes, which are passed down to the next generation. With consistent practice, you will experience mutation, reaching a phase in which you no longer need to worry about being influenced by external conditions.

When you practice with the aim of attaining nirvana, you will experience the four different stages. Many people in the first stage will be happy just to make it to the next stage. However, the ultimate goal of practice is to go beyond the third stage and reach the final fourth stage.

Like Water, Like Wind

Like water changing its form according to the shape of a bowl,
They accommodate others without insisting on their ways.
That is the state of Buddhahood.

Where are you in your practice? How far do you want to go in your practice? If your goal is to reach the second stage, you must change your current way of life. This requires a firm resolution. You must take decisive actions to restructure your current lifestyle and relationships. However, if you want to become like those in the third stage, you don't necessarily have to make a drastic change in your lifestyle. A strong determination is all you need. As long as you are certain of the personal values you want to uphold, you won't be swayed by what others around you say or do. When you look at a person who drinks, you should be able to say to yourself, "Whether that person drinks or not is his business."

However, when you are inclined toward the second stage, even when you don't have clearly defined values, it is possible to purify yourself by leaving society and only associating with people with good habits. Then, you can emulate their behavior and become like them. For example, if you live with people who wake up at 4 o'clock in the morning and turn on the lights, you have no choice but to wake up with them. External conditions inevitably force you to adjust your behavior accordingly. On the other hand, if you belong to the third stage, you have full control of yourself regardless of your environment.

External conditions are very important factors in shaping the lives of people in the first stage. It is not an exaggeration to assume that external conditions are the determining influence in their lives. On the other hand, for those in the second stage, the kind of place they choose to practice is very important. So they naturally talk about which mountain, which dharma teacher, and which country would be ideal for their practice. Like the people in the first category who roam the world seeking a comfortable life, an ideal spouse, a good job, and an interesting field of study, those in the second category also search for good people, places, and books in the name of seeking "the Truth."

The people in the first stage love to indulge in eating and sleeping whenever they get a chance and have busy love lives; they basically try to enjoy life to the fullest. On the other hand, those in the second category are the opposite. They eat and sleep as sparingly as possible and try to stay away from the opposite gender.

However, those in the third category are like neither those in the first nor those in the second. They are indifferent to external conditions such as the locations or circumstances in which they practice. They are well aware that the root of all suffering is in the mind. Because of their firm belief, they neither try to avoid nor are enticed by external conditions. They do not care whether or not their neighbors live in a small or a big house, wake up early or late in the morning, and what they eat or do. These people think, "It's their life, so it's up to them. I live frugally because I like living this way. I don't have to either follow or reject the way others live."

The people in the second stage ridicule and look down upon those in the first stage, saying, "They are foolish and crazy. No wonder they are suffering." Unlike those in the second stage, the people in the third stage do not criticize the ones in the first stage. They mind their own business and think, "The people in the first stage are only acting that way because of their disposition and karma." This is not an indication of lack of compassion on the part of those in the third stage. These people simply believe that their practice does not depend on what others do.

The people in the fourth category don't dwell on their practice. Like water, which changes its shape according to the cup that holds it, they do not insist on a course of action but simply respond to each person and situation in an appropriate manner. In Buddhism, this manifestation is called "Hwajak." That is, in order to guide others toward the right path, Bodhisattvas transform themselves to embody billions of different beings most appropriate to the situations and the karmas of the people they encounter.

To give another example, those in the first category will respond by swearing right back at someone who swears at them. Those in the second category will avoid anyone who swears at them. Those in the third category will not get angry at a person who swears at them. However, those in the fourth category will not hesitate to swear back at the person for the purpose of helping him become enlightened. The difference is that those in the first category can't help swearing because they are upset at the people to whom they swear whereas those in the fourth category swear because they have a certain objective, not because they can't control their temper.

Fortunately, it is possible for those in the first category

to become like those in the fourth category. Even when you have responded angrily to the words of other people, if you can realize right away, "I responded emotionally and swore," and admit, "This is the state of my practice," you can consider it an experience that helps you in your practice. You don't need to feel embarrassed about your current state of practice. When you don't know something, you can always ask. Also, if you make a mistake, you can simply correct it. Finally, if you know that you did something wrong, you can repent right away.

Nothing to Be Attained

"There is nothing to be attained."
Knowing this truth,
One lets go of the desire to attain.

People often say "Give us freedom." But why do we want freedom? What kind of freedom are we talking about? Is freedom being able to do whatever we want to do?

At school, there are many occasions when the entire class goes to watch a movie together with the teachers. When the teacher announces, "We are going to the movies today," most students are happy but a few are not. One student may say to the teacher, "I don't want to go to the movies." In response, the teacher will most likely dismiss the remark and tell him that the entire class is required to go. However, if the student still doesn't want to participate in the event, he will protest to the teacher, "I have the right not to go to the movies."

Now, let's look at a different scenario. The same student is studying for an exam at home and suddenly feels the urge to go to the movies. He asks his mother for permission, but she doesn't allow him to go. He keeps on pestering his mother. Yet she doesn't give in. What do you think he will say to defend his position? He will most likely plead to his mother, "I have the right to go to the movies." Before, when there was a school trip to the movies, this student claimed he had "the right not to go to the movies." However, now that his mother forbids him from going to the movies before the exam, he asserts "the right to go to the movies." What does freedom mean to this student?

To him, freedom is not going to the movies when he doesn't want to and going to the movies when he does want to. At the root of his rationale is the belief that freedom is being able to do whatever he wants to do. However, as long as people define freedom this way, they can never enjoy complete freedom. In reality, we have the freedom to go to the movies or not go to the movies.

We have the right to smoke or not to smoke. When you are asked not to smoke during a dharma talk, you are not being stripped of your freedom to smoke but rather, you are exercising your right not to smoke. If someone holds you at gunpoint and demands that you smoke, you don't need to resist but casually enjoy the freedom to smoke. When people insist on smoking but don't have any cigarettes on them, they feel like they are being deprived of their right to smoke. On the other hand, for people insisting on not smoking, they will feel that their "freedom not to smoke" is violated when they are forced to smoke.

True freedom means being free under any circumstances. You can enjoy the right to smoke when you have to smoke, and you can also enjoy the right not to smoke when smoking is prohibited. When we reach the state of total freedom, we are free from any external hindrances. In this state, we can be happy whether or not we fall into the sea. In other words, if we are thrust into the sea by a big wave, we can enjoy the freedom of gathering clams, but if we do not fall into the sea, we can enjoy the freedom of sailing on a boat.

It is the same with marriage. People who are already married can enjoy the freedom of being married, and those who are single can enjoy the freedom of not being married. Once you realize this, you will feel free under any given circumstances. This is the kind of freedom no one can give you or take away from you.

To sum up, you need to let go of the idea that things must go your way. As long as you hold on to this belief, it is quite impossible for you to enjoy unhindered freedom. In the Heart Sutra, there is a phrase, "There is nothing to be attained." Knowing that, you can become a truly free person by letting go of your desire to attain things in life.

5

People · World · Nature

The world exists in our awareness
and we exist in the world.
Making the world better and becoming enlightened
cannot be separated.

Pure Land

A world in which nature is beautiful,
Society is peaceful and
Individuals are happy

Pure Land (Jungto) refers to a clean and idealistic world. Everyone in Pure Land has a pure mind. They are always happy, joyous, and live in harmony with one another. Pure Land is a world where nature is beautiful, society is peaceful and individuals are happy.

Pure Land can be divided into three large categories. The first is called Other-World Pure Land (Tabang Jungto). In the world in which we live, individuals are unhappy, society is chaotic, and the natural environment is polluted. Somewhere far away, however, there is a place where crops grow on their own, trees are full of fruits, clean water flows, and the land is covered with treasures. Not only is nature beautiful in this place, but also there is no fighting or conflict among people. There are no wars, no starvation, and no diseases.

In this world, the sound of the wind, the babble of flowing water, and the chirping of the birds all resonate the teachings of the Buddha; every sound is a reflection of his teachings. People always honor the Buddha, awaken to the principles of non-ego and non-form. They are solely interested in attaining enlightenment. Such a world exists in the East, West, South, North, in all the heavens above, and the earth below. This is Other-World Pure Land.

The Sukhavati Pure Land of the West best represents the Other-World Pure Land. It can be compared to Paradise or Heaven in Western culture. Amitabha is the resident Buddha of the Sukhavati Pure Land, and Bodhisattva Avalokitesvara helps him in guiding the unenlightened beings to the Other-World Pure Land. Thus, people pray to Avalokitesvara to help them make their journey to Sukhavati Pure Land, where they can meet Amitabha Buddha and attain enlightenment.

The Other-World Pure Land exists in a different spatial dimension but in the same time dimension as the one in which we live. It is believed that those who aspire to be reborn in the Sukhavati Pure Land are able to make their wishes come true by earnestly chanting the name of Amitabha Buddha.

Future World

When the world improves
And all unenlightened beings become free from suffering
Through my bodhisattva practices,
Only then will I attain Buddhahood.

The second category of Pure Land is the Future-World Pure Land. We do not need to try to find where Pure Land is because the world where we are living right now can become a Pure Land of the future. Once Maitreya (Future Buddha) descends to this world from Tusita Heaven (a heaven where all boddhisattvas, even Shakamuni Buddha, resided before their rebirth on Earth) individuals will be happy, society will be at peace, and natural disasters will disappear, making the world a beautiful Pure Land. The Maitreya Pure Land is Future-World Pure Land, which will someday manifest itself in the world we live.

However, in order to attain enlightenment by being born during the era when Maitreya descends to this world, you must conduct the ten virtuous deeds.

1. No matter how many people fight and kill one another, you yourself shall not kill.

2. No matter how many people steal, you yourself shall not steal.

3. No matter how many people engage themselves in sexual misconduct, you yourself shall not engage in such misconduct.

4. No matter how many people tell lies, you yourself shall not tell lies.

5. No matter how many people deceive with false stories, you yourself shall not deceive with such stories.

6. No matter how many people deliberately create discord with others by their speech, you yourself shall not use divisive speech.

7. No matter how many people get angry and hurt others with

harsh words, you yourself shall not use such words.

8. No matter how many people are greedy, you yourself shall not be greedy.

9. No matter how many people get angry, you yourself shall not get angry.

10. No matter how many people have mistaken views that ignore the principle of cause and effect, you yourself shall not fall into such views.

When people abstain from doing the ten bad deeds and actively perform good deeds, they can be born into the Future-World Pure Land.

What the Other-World Pure Land and the Future-World Pure Land have in common is that they both exist in reality, and they both have a set of specific conditions that make them Pure Land. Moreover, once these worlds are created by those who envisioned them, the creators can then attain enlightenment and become Buddhas themselves. Therefore, only when the world becomes a better place with our bodhisattva practices and all unenlightened beings become free of suffering, shall we attain Buddhahood.

The World, Beautiful Just the Way It Is

When anguish disappears from our minds,
The world is beautiful as it is.
When our minds are pure, the world is clean and pure.

The third is Within-Mind Pure Land. Pure Land does not exist in some other place or in the future. When anguish disappears from our minds, the current world in which we live becomes a beautiful place as it is. When our minds are pure, the world is clean and pure. This is called Within-Mind Pure Land. The moment we become enlightened, we realize that the world in which we live is actually Pure Land.

Why do people yearn for Pure Land? It is because they are unhappy and are not free in the present moment and place. They want to break free from their suffering and restrictions. If the cause of our suffering comes from something outside of ourselves, such as the environment and the society in which we live, that suffering disappears once we move to a place with better living conditions. It is true that, in reality, moving to a better place or avoiding the people with whom we have conflicts does relieve a lot of our suffering.

For instance, if someone were to move to Korea from a country like Somalia, they would no longer suffer from starvation. In this case, Korea would be Other-World Pure Land. In other words, if the sick and starving people from a third world country were to come to Korea and get regular meals and medical treatment, Korea would be Pure Land to them. Thus, it can be said Other-World Pure Land exists in our daily lives.

Although we may not be well off now, to hope for our

society to progress and become Pure Land is to dream of Future-World Pure Land. However, since the world does not get better by itself, we need to work together to make it into a better place. For example, if we make efforts in our lives such as repairing our dilapidated houses, working hard to earn a living, and marrying someone we love, then we will be happier than before. This is Future-World Pure Land.

However, you may have experienced situations in which your life improves just by changing your mindset, without any changes in time or place. Although all you did was change your attitude, the very same star seems to shine a little brighter, and the same leaves and rocks somehow feel totally different. The parents, children, husband, wife, friends, and colleagues with whom you have shared your life seem completely different. Even though nothing has actually changed, when your mindset changes in a positive direction, things seem different and better. This is Within-Mind Pure Land.

No single one among Other-World, Future-World, or

Within-Mind Pure Land can be said to be absolute because all three of the Pure Lands exist in this world. In fact, we can improve our lives if we move to a place with better social conditions, we can live fuller lives if we strive a little harder, and we can live happier lives if we alter our mindset.

The Pure Land envisioned in Buddhism is not separated into three different Pure Lands. Instead, believers yearn for a world in which Other-World, Future-World, and Within-World Pure Lands are integrated together. Everyone has a strong aspiration to make this world into a better place like the Future-World Pure Land. Everyone wants to live in an ideal place like the Other-World Pure Land.

On the other hand, if we cultivate our minds and are content with our current situations, this world is a Within-Mind Pure Land. None of these three Pure Lands are neither superior to nor in conflict with the other two. We should seek them simultaneously and continuously in our lives.

Awareness Revolution

The world exists in our awareness
And we exist in the world.
Thus, making the world better
And becoming enlightened cannot be separated.

People have their own individual wishes. They want to lead long and healthy lives, have their children become successful, and always be prosperous. They feel good when these wishes come true.

Then, is Pure Land a place where everyone's wishes come true? For example, if everyone's wishes of being elected into political office, being accepted to a prestigious university, and becoming the richest person in the world were all to come true, the world would surely fall into chaos. The irony is that we aim for the greatest happiness but end up inviting the deepest of sorrows.

If suffering is caused by social disorder, then social disorder must disappear for our suffering to end. And, in order for social disorder to disappear, individuals must control their desires. Ultimately, moderation and control of desires will lead to happiness. If we can view our world in its entirety, we will know how to live happier lives and realize why we keep falling into misfortune even when we are striving so hard to be happy.

To make this world into Pure Land, we first need to moderate and control our own desires. We then need to alter our value system by changing our lifestyle and standard of happiness. An awareness revolution, similar to the phenomena of mutation, needs to happen. In other words, we must become enlightened.

Our minds are deeply influenced by external conditions. We believe that if only the conditions had been good from the beginning, our minds would not have become so chaotic. We blame other people or circumstances when we get irritated or when something goes a little awry. In short, we blame the external conditions.

However, the world, which we label as the external condition, is made up of the sum of each one of us. Without us, there is no world. We live in this world, we learn from this world, and we give back to this world what we have learned. Our awareness is constantly interacting with the external world.

When the world changes, so does our awareness. When the world becomes a better place, so do we. Who, then, makes the world into a better place? In order to improve the world, we need people who are aware of the problems in the world. These are the enlightened people, and they need to make the world a better place.

If our world is to improve, we need an increasing

number of people with this awareness. Specifically, we need more enlightened people, who think, "This will not do. We need a different way of life." When one person becomes enlightened, the impact does not end with just that person. Since an enlightened person has a positive influence on the world, it will be easier for the next person to become enlightened. As a result, one person will soon turn into two, and two will quickly turn into ten. This way, the world will move little by little in the direction of Pure Land.

Because the world exists in our awareness and we exist in the world, making the world a better place and becoming enlightened cannot be separated. It is wrong to assert that it is fine for me to enjoy happiness because I am enlightened even though the world is chaotic. At the same time, it is also wrong to assert that there is no need to become enlightened because unless the world changes, I am destined to suffer. No matter how chaotic the world is, a mutation that transcends these problems can occur.

Once a mutation occurs, it cannot be contained. It

multiplies, influences, and changes the world a little at a time. Evolution does not happen simply with the passage of time. Evolution consists of the appearance of a sudden anomaly that becomes dominant. The mental realm evolves in the same way.

We need to have the opportunity to become awakened through practice and cultivation. Initially, this opportunity should be extended to one person. However, it should not stop with that one individual but should be spread throughout our society, creating opportunities for others to become enlightened. At first, individuals should be guided toward the path to enlightenment. Then, taking it further, social structure should be advanced and social atmosphere altered so that they are conducive to helping everyone attain enlightenment more easily.

Once this happens, the debate over whether an individual's awakening should occur before or after making the world a better place becomes irrelevant. These two things will always be realized together like the two sides of the same coin.

Pure Mind, Good Friends, and Clean Land

Only when you live, do I live.
Only when you are happy, am I happy.

Regardless of the quality of our life conditions, natural environment, or the society we live in, we find ourselves becoming lighthearted once we let go of our fixed ideas and thoughts. Although the world did not change and our situation is the same, our minds are at peace the moment we let go of our stubbornness. Our minds brighten up regardless of whether we lost our jobs, failed an exam, or lost our parents. What's more, everyone around us appears lovable. Those who frowned and swore at us in the past now seem charming, and even the leaves on the tree and the earthworms come across as precious. Enlightenment is a phenomenon that occurs to an individual abruptly. And, just as suddenly, it can disappear.

To sustain enlightenment, first, we should keep our minds pure by letting go of greed. Second, we should try to keep our minds cheerful. Ironically, there are more gloomy people who are prone to sadness and crying among good-natured people. This is because they are more emotionally attached to others. This does not mean that they should not be affectionate, but they should stop becoming overly attached to others and also try to maintain a cheerful disposition. Third, we should keep our minds flexible. We should not be trapped by our own thoughts. Our minds are heavy when we fixate on a certain thought. As such, keeping our minds pure, cheerful, and flexible is called "Pure Mind." We should always maintain this Pure Mind in our everyday lives.

However, it is difficult to maintain this enlightenment by ourselves. Therefore, people with pure minds should interact with one another in order to maintain and even synergistically enhance each other's state of enlightenment. That is, we should help enlighten other people and be enlightened by others. In this symbiotic relationship, when others are more enlightened, we become more enlightened; when others are happy, we become happy; and when others live, we are able to live. This is the concept of "Good Friends." Good Friends do not compete or fight with one another; they help one another. The more they interact with each other, the more they help each other, so the relationship continues to improve.

Whatever it may be, we should not keep things to ourselves, but instead, we should share with others. We should share our happiness as well as our suffering. When we openly share our happiness with others, and are willing to receive happiness from others, we can build more rewarding and meaningful relationships. We should be able to experience such closeness in our verbal exchange with people we meet at any time and place in our lives.

Our families, social organizations, and society as a whole must keep on evolving this way, so that those who are not as awakened may be positively influenced by the change in their communities. Furthermore, if such change becomes a social trend, any child born into that society will naturally model themselves after the good examples around him. A society should be made up of the kind of people described in the concept of Good Friends.

A delicious snack won't taste as good if you hoard it and eat it by yourself. Owning something valuable won't give you much pleasure if there is no one around to appreciate it with you. People feel happy when they exchange compliments and recognize one another. Having each other makes all the difference and makes life seem that much better. Our lives should evolve in order to create this kind of ideal community. The spirit of friends helping one another should be reflected not only in our families but also everywhere else, including our workplaces, our societies, and even our countries.

Currently, we are destroying our environment in the name of development so that we can live better by consuming more. Ironically, the measures that we took to improve our lives have ended up polluting the air, the water, and the food we intake. Now, our world has become an unsafe place where we worry about the lack of safe food, pure water, and clean air.

No matter what development policy we adopt, it should be implemented without destroying the environment. Economic growth is only sustainable when the pace of development stays within nature's ability to regenerate.

We must not lose sight of the Law of Interdependence, which gives us the fundamental perspective, "I can live only when you live." Since the environment is so vital to our survival, we need to save and preserve the environment at all costs by keeping our lands clean and nature unharmed. Nature is not an object of human conquest. Actually, it is what enables us to continue living. Thus, a harmonious and balanced relationship must be maintained between humanity and nature.

Returning to the Fundamental Teachings of the Buddha

If we return to the Buddha's fundamental teachings
And practice "Right Buddhism," "Simple Buddhism,"
And "Everyday Buddhism,"
We can attain liberation and nirvana
Even in our everyday lives.

The contemporary Korean Buddhism deviates significantly from Buddha's fundamental principles. For example, prayers such as "Bless my children," or "Grant me longevity," cannot fundamentally alleviate the suffering in our lives. To root out our suffering, we need to return to the basic teachings of the Buddha and recover the true faith of

Buddhism.

Monks and lay Buddhists alike must return to the fundamental ideals of Buddhism. It's not enough that only a few Buddhist monks devote themselves to the right Buddhist practice, while lay Buddhists are left to practice however they want. All Buddhists should return to the basic teachings of the Buddha. This is "Right Buddhism."

Right Buddhism refers to getting rid of fixed notions and always seeing the truth of the dharma. This includes not deviating from the fundamental teachings of the Buddha. We must not lose sight of enlightenment by settling for the status quo or being overly concerned with attaining merits.

However, if we insist on the theoretics of the fundamental Buddhist principles such as non-self, non-form, and emptiness, Buddhism will come across as esoteric to most people. In order to overcome this problem, Buddha taught with various methods according to the individual's predisposition. As a result, the Buddha's teachings enabled men and women of all ages, each under various different circumstances, to eventually arrive at the truth. Therefore, fundamental Buddhism should begin by first solving the real problems of each person. This is "Easy Buddhism."

In reality, if the emphasis is on the fundamental doctrines, Buddhism runs the risk of becoming a religion led by just an elite few. On the other hand, if the emphasis is on the populace, Buddhism may end up blindly following public demands, lose sight of the fundamentals, and take a path towards secularization.

We also need to be wary of the belief that the truth is irrelevant to and separate from our everyday lives. This belief prevents us from incorporating Buddhism into our everyday lives. Leaving the secular world does not mean an end to our social life. Because the teachings of the Buddha can be found in our daily routines of eating meals, going to school, working at our jobs, and doing housework, our practice should begin right where we live. This is "Everyday Buddhism."

Anyone who goes back to the Buddha's fundamental

teachings and practices "Right Buddhism," "Easy Buddhism," and "Everyday Buddhism" can attain liberation and nirvana in his daily life.

Cultivators of Pure Land

The one who practices, gives, and volunteers
The one who is resolved to build Pure Land in this world
The one who lives to realize this aspiration

How should someone practice if he is determined to build Pure Land in this world? First, he should begin doing practice, even by himself. However, it is better to practice together with other like-minded people.

Furthermore, if he can practice with others, including the ones with conflicting views, this is an act of a Bodhisattva. The act of a Bodhisattva is to simply practice regardless of whether or not other people in the world give support and follow suit. Such practice benefits others and lays the foundation for them to get to Pure Land.

In Bodhisattva practice, first, one needs to discipline his own mind. This is the essence of practice. The act of Bodhisattva not only puts one's own mind at ease but also aims to benefit others. In other words, the act of Bodhisattva is to give. It should not end, however, with sharing your wealth but should also extend to sharing your talents to help others. This is to volunteer.

There is no fixed order in which practicing, giving, and volunteering should be done. If you do not respond in anger when someone swears at you, it is "to practice." If you provide a meal to a hungry person, it is "to give." If you help a child up when he falls down, it is "to volunteer."

We practice, give, and volunteer in order to build Pure Land. Those who aspire to build Pure Land in this world and live to make their aspiration come true are the true cultivators of Pure Land. They follow the Bodhisattva way by practicing, giving, and volunteering in their everyday lives.

A Bodhi Tree Seed

There are two seeds. One is a bean and the other is a Bodhi tree seed. Outwardly, they are similar in shape and size. However, the hidden potential of these two seeds is very different. A bean sprouts, grows, and then withers in less than a year. A Bodhi tree seed, however, continues to mature and grow into a big tree that provides people with a place to rest for many years to come.

We can compare these two seeds to the kinds of work we choose to do. If we seek small profits, we will be just like the annual bean vine that quickly blooms, bears fruit, and withers within a year's cycle. However, if our aspiration is genuine and steadfast, no matter how insignificant it may seem in the beginning, it will become like the Bodhi tree that gives great help to a countless number of people.

I sincerely hope that this book will be like a Bodhi tree seed. I pray that it reaches people I have never met in places I have never been and grows into a grand Bodhi tree.

About the Author

Venerable Pomnyun Sunim is a Korean Buddhist monk who is the founder and leading Zen master of the Jungto Society. He entered the Buddhist Sangha at Boonwhangsa Temple, South Korea, in 1969, and was ordained a bihikku in 1991.

He is not only a Buddhist monk but also a social activist who leads various movements such as an ecological awareness campaign, promotion of human rights and world peace, and eradication of famine, disease, and illiteracy.

Ven. Pomnyun Sunim has been advocating a new paradigm of civilization movement in which everyone becomes happy through practice, creates a happy society through active participation in social movements, and protects our environment and the Earth by adopting a simple lifestyle. This vision is expressed in the Jungto Society's motto, "Open Mind, Good Friends, and Clean Earth."

Instead of lecturing about Buddhism, he invites individuals in his audience to ask him questions about their concerns and doubts. He then engages them in a dialogue to help them gain insight into the true nature of their problems with his extraordinary gift for explaining the Buddha's teachings in simple layman's terms. He challenges them to question their personal biases and helps them become more aware of their own perception of the world. After a short exchange with Ven. Pomnyun Sunim, most people are able to view their problems in a different light and feel happier and freer in their lives.

His talks have become very popular over the years and it is not unusual to see an audience of 2,000 or more people at his talks in Korea. His "Hope" speaking tour from 2011 until 2014 was attended by more than 600,000 participants across 436 locations in Korea. In 2014, he went on a global speaking tour. He visited 106 cities around the world in 114 days and delivered 115 talks to more than 20,000 Koreans living overseas. Of these 115 talks, 8 were conducted in English for English-speaking audiences.

Pomnyun Sunim's words of wisdom can be accessed through his books, social media, YouTube, TV, and radio. He has published more than 50 books since 1994. His latest book, "The Moment of Enlightenment," published in January 2015, became the #1 bestseller in Korea within two weeks of publication. He has over 1 million followers in Korea's KakaoTalk, 100,000 daily downloads of his podcasts, and over 3 million views of his YouTube videos.

His extensive humanitarian work includes efforts to alleviate the suffering of ordinary North Koreans through the development of food aid programs and by working with marginalized people in Asian countries to build schools and promote community development. In recognition of his humanitarian work, he received the Ramon Magsaysay Award for Peace and International Understanding in 2002 and the POSCO TJ Park Community Development and Philanthropy Prize in 2011. Finally, in 2015, Pomnyun Sunim received Kripasaran Award from the Bengal Association at the 150th Birth Anniwversary Celebration of Ven. Mahasthavir Kripasaran, for his efforts in reviving Buddhism in India.

Other Books by the Author

- Korean*

Engaged Buddhism

Buddhism and Environment

Buddhism and Peace

Peace of Mind, Compassionate Society

The Beautiful Harmony of Work and Practice

Commentary on the Heart Sutra

Lecture on the Diamond Sutra

The Buddha

The Way to the Unification of the Korean Peninsula

The New Century: Envisioning Reunification

Words of Wisdom for Newlyweds

Lessons for Mothers

Lessons for Life

The Moment of Enlightenment

* The complete list of Ven. Pomnyun Sunim's publications in Korean is available at www.jungtosociety.org

- English

True Happiness

True Freedom

True Wisdom

Prayer

- French

La Famille

- Japanese
Happy Commute to Work
Ask, If You Want to Know

- Chinese
Happy Commute to Work
A House Filled with Laughter

- Thai
Happy Commute to Work

Awards

1998 Kyobo Environmental Education Award, Korea
2000 Manhae Propagation Award, Korea
2002 Ramon Magsaysay Peace and International Understanding Award, Philippines
2006 DMZ(Demilitarized Zone)Peace Prize, Gangwon Province, Korea
2007 National Reconciliation and Cooperation Award, Korean
       Council for Reconciliation and Cooperation, Korea
2011 POSCO TJ Park Community Development and Philanthropy Prize,
       POSCO Chungam Foundation, Korea
2011 Reunification and Culture Award, Reunification and Culture
       Research Institute, Segye Daily, Korea
2015 Kripasaran Award, the Bengal Association, India

Jungto Society, a Community Based on Buddhist Practice

The Jungto Society was founded by Ven. Pomnyun Sunim with the aim of building a community of Buddhists who practice together and aspire to solve the problems of poverty, political and social conflicts, and environmental degradation.

While placing emphasis on personal transformation through individual practice, the Jungto Society has actively participated in various social movements such as the protection of the environment; eradication of famine, disease and illiteracy; advocacy of peace and human rights; and the unification of the Korean peninsula.

Ven. Pomnyun Sunim and the members of the Jungto Society look into the 2,500-year-old teachings of the Buddha to find solutions for modern problems of this world. They have been the forerunners in various projects to help people around the world including North Korea and many Third World countries. As of 2015, the Jungto Society consists of 116 regional chapters in Korea and 21 overseas chapters including 11 in the United States.

About the Jungto Overseas Translation Team

The Jungto Overseas Translation Team is a group of volunteers attending Jungto Society near their homes in various cities around the world. Although the members vary in profession, gender and age, they share the common experience of having their lives transformed by the wisdom they found in Ven. Pomnyun Sunim's dharma talks.

Currently, one group of the Jungto Overseas Translation Team is translating the large selection of Pomnyun Sunim's Youtube videos into English, while another group living in Europe is translating them into French. With the increase in the number of translated videos, Pomnyun Sunim's wisdom is expected to reach a wider audience and help people all over the world to live a life of freedom and happiness.